This Book Belongs To

Joe Casey

Text copyright © 2001 Margaret Ryan
Illustrations copyright © 2001 David Melling

First published in 2001
by Hodder Children's Books

A Catalogue record for this book is available from the
British Library

ISBN 0 340 77937 3

Printed and bound in Great Britain
by Omnia Books Limited, Glasgow

Hodder Children's Books
A Division of Hodder Headline Limited
338 Euston Road, London NW1 3BH

Bumpy's Rumbling Tummy

Written by Margaret Ryan

Illustrated by David Melling

Hodder
Children's
Books

a division of Hodder Headline Limited

To Ellie Louise
with love —
Margaret Ryan

For Sabina —
David Melling

Bumpy, the sun bear, was fast asleep in a big tree.

snuffle snuffle,
snore snore

Then she began to dream about honey. Lots and lots of honey.

"Thick honey, sweet honey
Very good to eat honey,"
she sang in her sleep.

Suddenly she heard a loud
rumbling noise. She woke
up fast.

"What's that?" she cried.
"Is it thunder?"

She looked up at the sky.
It was blue. There were no
black thunderclouds.

So Bumpy put her head back down on her paws and went back to sleep.

snuffle snuffle,
snore snore

This time she dreamed about juicy fruit. Lots and lots of juicy fruit.

"Red fruit, green fruit
Very good to eat fruit,"
she sang in her sleep.

Suddenly she heard a very
loud rumbling noise.
She woke up fast.

"What's that?" she cried.
"Is it Big Daddy Orang-utan?"

She looked through the trees.
They were empty. There was no
Big Daddy Orang-utan.

So Bumpy put her head back
down on her paws and went
back to sleep.

snuffle snuffle,
snore snore

This time she dreamed about
juicy fruit covered in honey.
Lots and lots of fruit and honey.

"Honey and fruit, fruit and honey.
That's what I like in my tummy,"

she sang in her sleep.

Suddenly she heard a very, very loud rumbling noise. Then another and another. She woke up fast.

"I know what that noise is," she cried. "It's not thunder. It's not Big Daddy Orang-utan. It's my tummy rumbling. I must give it some food right away!"

She bumped down from the tree
she was in . . .

. . . and climbed up another one.

She peeked through all the
leaves. She peeked through all
the branches.

She even peeked into holes in the trunk. But there was no honey.

"I'll just have to try another tree," said Bumpy.

She was just about to bump
down to the ground when her
jungle friend, Fuzzbuzz, the little
orang-utan, came swinging
through the trees.

"Hi, Bumpy," he said. "I'm going
to the river to make a raft.
I'm going to sail away and have
lots of adventures. Do you want
to come?"

"Sorry, Fuzzbuzz," said Bumpy.
"But my tummy's rumbling and
I'm too busy looking for honey
right now. I'm going to look in
that tall tree over there."

She bumped down from the tree
she was in . . .

. . . and climbed up another one.

BZZZZZZZZZZ

BZZZZZZZZZ

BZZZZZZZZZ

She met some busy bees.
"Buzz off, Bumpy," they buzzed.
"Keep your sticky paws off
our honey."

But Bumpy just grinned and
began to eat the honey. She ate
and ate and ate and sang herself
a little song . . .

"Thick honey, sweet honey
Very good to eat honey."

"That honey was yummy," she
said when she had finished. "But
there's still room in my tummy. I
must go and look for more food."

She bumped down from the tree
she was in . . .

. . . and landed right beside her jungle friend, Smiler, the crocodile. "Good morning, Bumpy," said Smiler. "I'm going to the river to help Fuzzbuzz make a raft. We're going to sail away and have lots of adventures. Do you want to come?"

"Sorry, Smiler," said Bumpy. "But my tummy's still rumbling and I'm too busy looking for juicy fruit right now. I think there might be some up in that tall tree over there."

And she climbed up
and up and up.

SCREEEEEECH
SCREEEEEECH
SCREEEEEECH!

She met some munching
monkeys.
"Scoot scram scoot, Bumpy,"
they muttered. "Keep your
sticky paws off our fruit."

But Bumpy just grinned, and began to eat the fruit. She ate and ate and ate and sang herself a little song . . .

"Red fruit, green fruit
Very good to eat fruit."

"That fruit was yummy," she said
when she had finished. "But
there's still room in my tummy. I
must go and look for more food."

She bumped down from the tree
she was in . . .

. . . and landed right beside
her jungle friend, Rainbow,
the parrot.

"Hi ya, Bumpy, old jungle friend.
I was in the bat cave chatting to
the bats, then I met Fuzzbuzz
and Smiler. I'm going to the river
to help them make a raft.
We're going to sail away and
have lots of adventures. Do you
want to come?"

"Sorry, Rainbow," said Bumpy.
"But my tummy's still rumbling,
and I'm too busy looking for
honey and juicy fruit right now.
I think there might be some up
in those tall trees over there."

And she climbed up and up
and up.

"Buzz off, Bumpy,"
buzzed the bees.

"Scoot scram scoot,
Bumpy," muttered
the monkeys.

But Bumpy just grinned and
began to eat and eat and eat.
She was just about to sing herself
a little song about honey and
fruit when she heard another
rumbling noise . . .

She looked
up at the sky,
but there were
no black
thunderclouds
or lightning.

She looked
through the
trees, but
it wasn't
Big Daddy
Orang-utan.

She looked down at her tummy, but it was full and fat and quiet.

"Oh no," she said. "It's the Angry Ant Gang. And they look hungry too!"

They were. They were marching
and chanting . . .

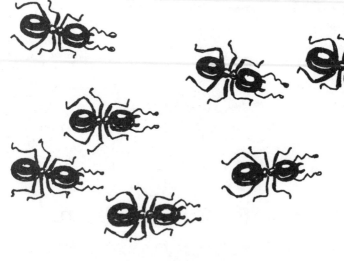

**"HERE WE COME,
GET OUT OF OUR WAY.
WE WANT FRUIT AND HONEY
AND WE WANT IT TODAY."**

"Oh no," cried Bumpy again.
"They're climbing up the tree to
get at the food. I'll have to jump
down into the river before they
sting me."

So she jumped . . .

WHEEE!

And landed . . . **BUMP** . . .
not in the river, but right on
the edge of the raft Fuzzbuzz
and Smiler
and Rainbow
were
making . . .

OUCH!

Up went the raft.
Up went Fuzzbuzz,
Smiler, and Rainbow.

Down came the raft. Down came
Fuzzbuzz, Smiler and Rainbow
into the river . . .

**WHEE! SPLISH!
SPLOOOOOOOSH!**

"Oops!" grinned Bumpy.
"I think you've just had your
first adventure!"